Young children can be overwhelmed by their emotions—often because they don't understand and can't express what they are feeling. This, in turn, can frustrate parents. After all, how can you help your child deal with a problem if you don't even share a common vocabulary?

Welcome to **HoW i FEEL** —a series designed to bridge this communication gap. With simple text, lively illustrations, and an interactive format, each book describes familiar situations to help children recognize a particular emotion. It gives them a vocabulary to talk about what they're feeling, and it offers practical suggestions for dealing with those feelings.

Each time you read this book with your child you can reinforce the message with one of the following activities:

- Ask your child to make up a story about a little girl or boy who feels jealous.

- Do some role playing. Act out situations that make your child feel jealous.

- Use the "Green-Eyed Jealousy Monster" activity included in this book to help your child explore different causes and different degrees of jealousy.

I hope you enjoy the **HoW i FEEL** series and that it will help your child take the first solid steps toward understanding emotions.

Marcia Leonard

Executive Producers: John Christianson and Ron Berry
Art Design: Gary Currant
Layout: Currant Design Group and Best Impression Graphics

JEALOUS

by Marcia Leonard
illustrated by Bartholomew

This little boy's big sister
is going to a party with her friends.
He feels jealous.

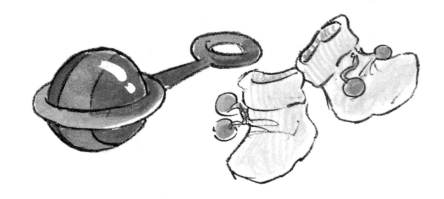

This little girl feels jealous, too.
Her parents are paying attention
to the new baby—not to her.

These kids are jealous because
someone else gets to be first in line.

Has that ever happened to you?
Can you make a face that looks jealous?

You might feel jealous
if someone has a toy that you want.

Have you ever felt that way?

Or you might feel jealous
if your best friend
plays with someone else.

Would that make you jealous?

Jealousy can be a big, angry feeling.
It can be a sad, hurt feeling.
It is never a comfortable feeling.
So how can you make it go away?

Sometimes it helps
if you make your own fun.

Sometimes, if you ask nicely,
kids will let you share their toys
or join in their game.

And sometimes all you need to do
is be patient and wait your turn.

But if your jealous feelings don't go away,
you should talk to Mommy or Daddy,
because they can help you
feel comfortable again.

Instructions

Use this activity to help your child explore the cause and intensity of his or her jealousy. Remove the card and reusable stickers from the back pocket of the book. Ask your child to choose a sticker that represents a situation that makes him or her jealous and place it on the card. Explain that jealousy is often described as a "green-eyed monster" because it can grow into a big, mean feeling. Then help your child use the monster stickers to cover up the figure on the card—a little or a lot, depending on how jealous he or she feels. Does your child feel a tiny bit jealous when someone else gets attention? Give the figure monster feet. Extremely jealous? Turn the figure into a full-fledged monster. Talk to your child about his or her feelings and about how to make the jealousy monster disappear.